For Jane, Hannah and Joe – M.M.

For Chris – E.G.

First published 2021 by Two Hoots
This edition published 2022 by Two Hoots
an imprint of Pan Macmillan
The Smithson
6 Briset Street
London
EC1M 5NR
EU representative: Macmillan Publishers Ireland Limited, 1st Floor,
The Liffey Trust Centre, 117–126 Sheriff Street Upper, Dublin 1, D01 YC43

Associated companies throughout the world
www.panmacmillan.com
ISBN: 978-1-5290-6332-5
Text copyright © Michael Morpurgo 2021
Illustrations copyright © Emily Gravett 2021
Moral rights asserted.

Music from 'Flight' on pages 2 and 33 copyright © Rachel Portman 2020, reproduced by kind permission
A version of this story first appeared in *The Book of Hopes*, edited by Katherine Rundell,
published by Bloomsbury Publishing plc

1 3 5 7 9 8 6 4 2

A CIP catalogue record for this book is available from the British Library.
Printed in China
The illustrations in this book were created using pencil and watercolour
with a smidgen of digital fiddle faddling

www.twohootsbooks.com

FSC
www.fsc.org
MIX
Paper from
responsible sources
FSC® C116313

MICHAEL MORPURGO · EMILY GRAVETT

A Song of Gladness

TWO HOOTS

I'VE BEEN TALKING
every morning to blackbird,
    telling him why we are all so sad.
    He sits on his branch and listens.

It was blackbird's idea. He sang it out this morning
at dawn from his treetop in the garden, to fox half asleep
behind the garden shed. She thought it a good idea too.
It was a wake-up call. Fox was on her feet at once, and
trotting through Bluebell Wood, where she barked it to
deer who ran off across the stream.

Kingfisher was there, otter and dipper too.
They heard, and piped it on, and swallow
swooped down over the meadow,

and passed it on to cows waiting to go in to their milking, and to sheep resting quietly under the hedge with her lambs in the corner of the dew-damp field.

And they all agreed, bleating it out to bees already busy at their flowers, to weaving spiders, and grasshoppers, and scurrying mice.

Trees were listening too, all the trees, waving their budding leaves in wild enthusiasm.

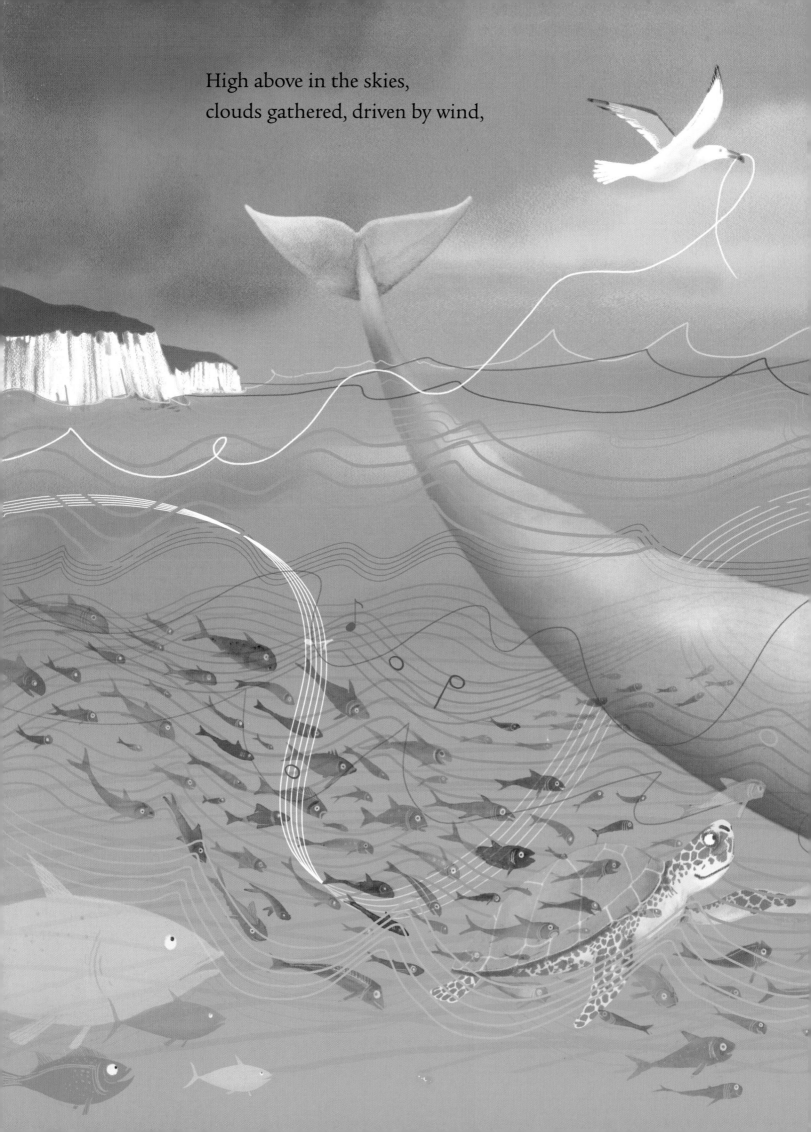

High above in the skies,
clouds gathered, driven by wind,

and wind took blackbird's idea over the cliffs across heaving seas,
where gulls and albatross cried it out, and whales and dolphins
and porpoises heard it, and wailed and whooped it down into
the deep, where turtles listened. And they too loved the idea.

So did plankton and every fish and crab and sea urchin
and whelk. They all whispered that it was a fine notion,
the best they ever heard.

In rivers, salmon and sea trout leapt for joy to hear it. Eagles soaring above on wide wings flew over the mountains crying it out loud, and the echoes were heard deep in the dens below, where slumbering bears listened, lost in their dreams of spring. They snored and grunted their approval, even in their sleep.

Snows melted at the thought of it, and the whole wonderful idea flooded down the mountain streams and far out to sea,

where the tide took it and carried it over the sea on curling
waves to distant shores, to parched plains, where lions roared
their approval, and elephants trumpeted it, leopards yawned it,

water buffalo belched it, wild dogs yelped it.
And wildebeest murmured it out across the wide savannah.

Then storm lifted the idea up over rainforests,
where rain took it and poured it down on gorillas
in the mist, on chimpanzees in their sleeping nests.

And crocodile swished his tail in his swamp, and clapped his great jaws shut, smiling at the very thought of it.

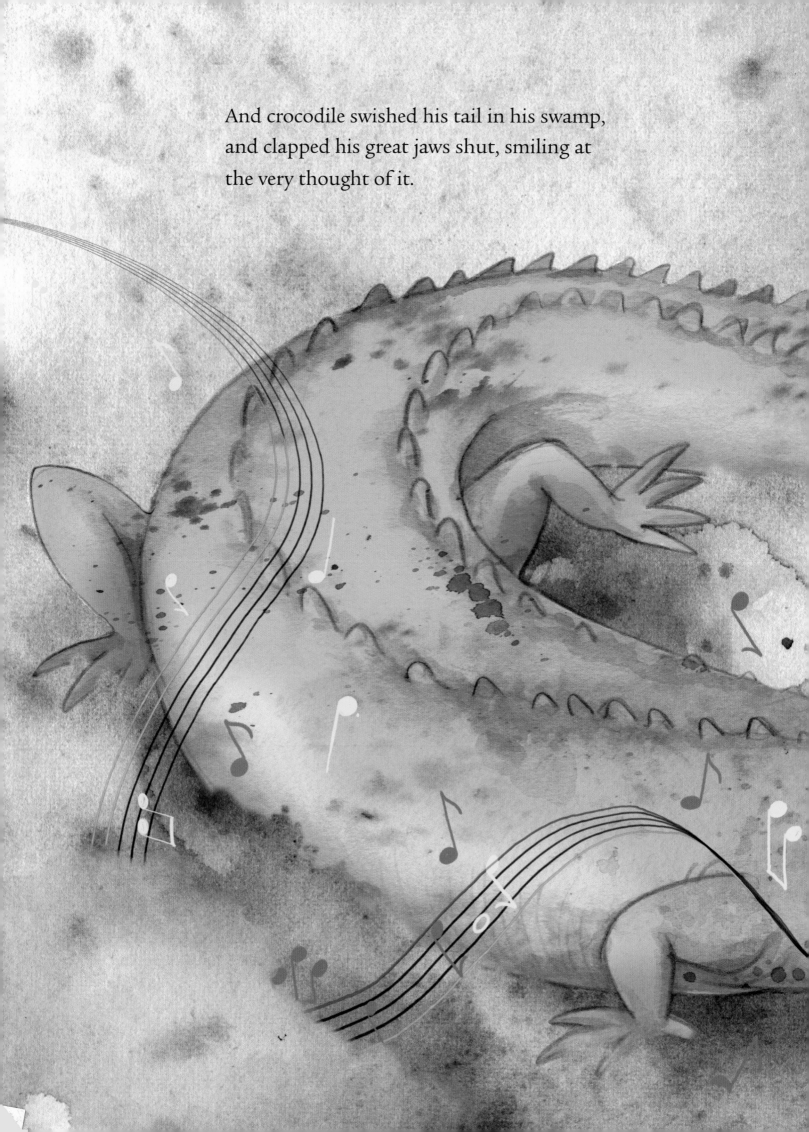

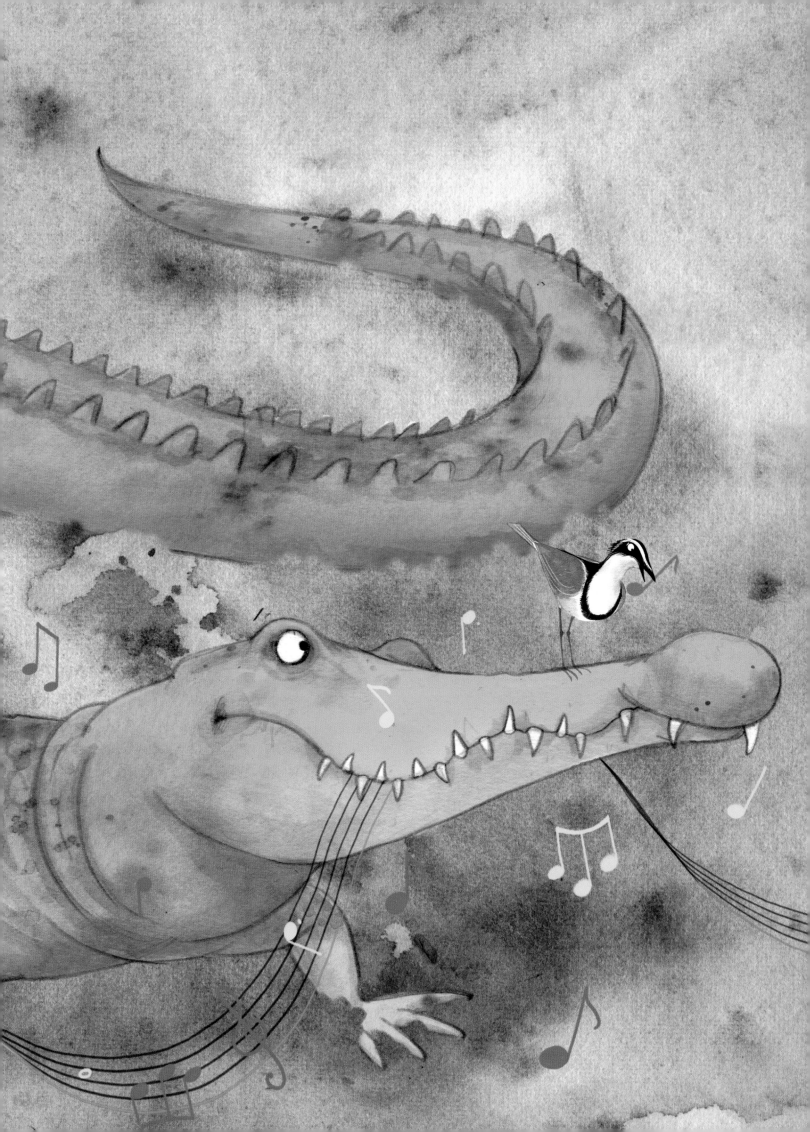

Howler monkeys and gibbons echoed their calls loud over all the earth – they are that loud; and then from far up high, sun heard it too and shone it down over deserts where oryx stamped her foot, impatient to be getting on with it and doing it – she loved the idea that much.

Even camel, who rarely joined in anything, thought this was the best and most beautiful idea he had ever heard.

Back in the garden,
blackbird waited till everyone was ready.

And then he began to sing. The whole carnival of animals
heard him and every living thing on this good earth joined in,
until the globe echoed with the joy of it.

Blackbird was very pleased.

But I was still lost in sadness, as I heard the earth singing around me. It was a song of forgiveness. I knew that. So I asked blackbird if I was allowed to join in. And he sang his answer back to me.

"My friend, why do you think we are doing this? We want you and yours to be happy again. Only then will you treat us and the world right, as you know you should. Only then will all be well. Sing, my friend, sing. Our song is your song, your song is our song."

So I sang, we all sang, sang away our sadness.

In every house and flat and cottage, we clapped and sang, in every shelter and tent, in every palace and hospital and prison. And they heard and we heard, our song of gladness echoing about us, in glorious harmony across the universe.

And one more thing...

For some years now I've been going out early every morning into the vegetable garden to pick kale or spinach, raspberries or gooseberries (my favourite). I was out there one lovely bright morning in March 2020, the year all of us will remember for the rest of our lives, a time of such sorrows.

There was not a cloud in the sky and all about me a silence so intense that I could hear it. The world seemed to have stopped. I felt I was alone on the planet. There was such beauty all around me, such peace. I should have been happy on such a morning, but instead I was overwhelmed with sadness.

Then a blackbird began to sing.

I knew at once he was singing to me, that this was personal. Sensing his welcome, I sang back, echoing his song. We had a conversation. It sounds fanciful. At first, I thought it was fanciful. But when he was there waiting for me, singing for me, every morning, I knew he was trying to get to know me, to tell me something, something important – urgent even.

He was telling me a story, singing a song he wanted the whole world to sing, every living creature on the planet.